SNOWBOARDING
SURPRISE

BY JAKE MADDOX

TEXT BY EMMA CARLSON BERNE
ILLUSTRATED BY KATIE WOOD

STONE ARCH BOOKS
a capstone imprint

Jake Maddox is published by Stone Arch Books, an imprint of Capstone.
1710 Roe Crest Drive
North Mankato, Minnesota 56003
www.capstonepub.com

Library of Congress Cataloging-in-Publication Data
Names: Berne, Emma Carlson, 1979- author. | Wood, Katie, 1981- illustrator. | Maddox, Jake. Jake Maddox girl sports stories.
Title: Snowboarding surprise / text by Emma Carlson Berne ; illustrated by Katie Wood. Description: North Mankato, Minnesota : Stone Arch Books, an imprint of Capstone, 2022. | Series: Jake Maddox girl sports stories | Audience: Ages 8-11. | Audience: Grades 4-6. | Summary: Samira has never been the best gymnast on her team, but she has always worked hard and loved what she was doing; but when a torn rotator cuff sidelines her and six months later her shoulder just does not seem to feel right—she discovers snowboarding, a whole new world of speed and excitement opens up before her, and Samira has to decide which sport to commit to.
Identifiers: LCCN 2021008476 (print) | LCCN 2021008477 (ebook) | ISBN 9781663910875 (hardcover) | ISBN 9781663921925 (paperback) | ISBN 9781663910844 (pdf) Subjects: LCSH: Snowboarding—Juvenile fiction. | Gymnastics—Juvenile fiction. | Sports injuries—Juvenile fiction. | Decision making—Juvenile fiction. | CYAC: Snowboarding—Fiction. | Gymnastics—Fiction. | Sports injuries—Fiction. | Decision making—Fiction. | LCGFT: Sports fiction. Classification: LCC PZ7.B455139 Sn 2021 (print) | LCC PZ7.B455139 (ebook) | DDC 813.6 [Fic]—dc23
LC record available at https://lccn.loc.gov/2021008476
LC ebook record available at https://lccn.loc.gov/2021008477

Designer: Bobbie Nuytten

TABLE OF CONTENTS

CHAPTER 1
Off Balance 5

CHAPTER 2
Bad News First 12

CHAPTER 3
Thanks, But No Thanks 19

CHAPTER 4
Slalom Slopes 29

CHAPTER 5
Gym Jitters...35

CHAPTER 6
Stick It! 40

CHAPTER 7
Back on the Board..47

CHAPTER 8
At Home on the Powder 55

CHAPTER 1

OFF BALANCE

Samira poised herself on the balance beam. Looking down the beam like this always reminded her of looking down a runway. She was the plane, about to take off. All around her, the gym echoed with the thumps, grunts, and staccato shouts of her team practicing.

Samira inhaled the chalky, rubber-scented air and dipped her hands forward for a handstand. She lifted her legs delicately, one by one, just like Coach Hosseni had taught her. "As if you're holding a glass between your feet," she always said.

Samira lowered to a backbend and then flipped to a double round-off. This would be the beginning of her new beam routine. Then she would move into a back walkover, a straight-leg leap, and dismount. She'd perform it for the first time at the Midwest Regionals next month.

Samira stretched her legs back behind her head, feeling the pull in her abdominal muscles. The hard surface of the beam met her feet, and she flipped upward and swung her legs back up over her head for the round-off.

But the beam wasn't there. Her body swung awkwardly to the left. She could tell immediately the move was off. The next thing she knew, she awkwardly slid off the beam and onto the mat.

"At least you fell gracefully," Samira's best friend Penelope said, running over from the vault.

Samira sighed, staring down at the blue vinyl mat. "It's *this* that's the problem." She grabbed her thighs. "Messing with my balance."

Penelope nodded solemnly. "Legs. Definitely a problem. Very hard to balance with legs. But harder to balance *without* legs."

Samira smiled but only a little. "You know what I mean. If I was built more like *that*, I wouldn't overcorrect like I just did." She gestured at Elise Klein who was short and wiry.

"Yeah, but if you were, you wouldn't rock the vault like you do." Penelope hauled Samira to her feet. "She doesn't have that powerful run you have."

"That's right, Penelope," Coach Hosseni said, coming over to them. "There's nothing wrong with your body, Samira. Everyone has their own shape and talents."

The coach gestured to herself. "Take me, for example," she said. "My sister and I were both gymnasts. She was short and wiry. I was taller and thicker. I had to work harder than my sister to do the same moves. But I really wanted it, so I didn't give up. My sophomore year, I won the state Junior All-Around. I did it, and you can too." Coach gave both girls a warm smile. "Now, I see that Jade is about to do her vault approach, so let me help her and you girls keep working."

"Well, I'm not giving up either," Samira told Penelope. "So my body had better figure it out!"

"It will. *You* will," Penelope reassured her. "I know you can."

Samira gave her friend a hug. "Thanks. What would I do without you?" She mounted the beam again and kept practicing.

Handstand. Backbend. Then the flip to a round-off. Samira gave an extra hard push through her arms as she squeezed the beam with her hands. It was *too* hard of a push. Her legs lifted, she felt that instant of weightlessness, but even before her feet smacked the beam squarely and perfectly, she felt a bolt of pain slam through her shoulder. Samira attempted to lift her arms, but the pain was too much. Gasping, she dropped from the beam.

"That was perfect! Wait—what's wrong?" Penelope asked.

Samira cradled her arm. "Oh shoot! Oh no! My shoulder."

Coach Hosseni jogged across the mats. With calm, practiced fingers, she rotated Samira's shoulder. When Samira cried out with pain again, Coach helped her to the bench.

"I'll call your parents," Coach said. "We need to get that looked at as soon as possible."

She left to get her phone, and Samira and Penelope stared at each other glumly. They knew as well as anyone what Coach wasn't saying. There weren't going to be any regionals for Samira—not now.

CHAPTER 2

BAD NEWS FIRST

"Well, I have got good news and bad news," Dr. Floyd said as she came into the exam room.

"Let's have the good news first," Samira's dad said.

"Can I have the bad news first, actually?" Samira asked. She cradled her arm across her chest in a black cloth sling.

"Sure," Dr. Floyd said. She sat down on a small, wheeled stool and opened a manila folder. "The bad news is you've got a rotator cuff tear. You'll need to rest it for six weeks, then start rehab."

"So I can go back to the gym after six weeks?" Samira asked. That wouldn't be too bad. She could do that.

Dr. Floyd looked up with a grimace on her face. Samira's dad reached over and took her hand. "No. Sorry, I should have been clearer. You can't do any gymnastics for at least six months. Your shoulder just can't handle the weight and the twisting and stretching."

"Oh," Samira whispered. It was hard to talk around the lump in her throat. "So . . . what's the good news?"

Dr. Floyd shut the folder with a snap and stood up. "The good news is that you can return to gymnastics eventually."

She said it brightly. "This injury won't end your gymnastics career, Samira."

Samira tried not to scowl.

Her dad cleared his throat. "Thank you, Dr. Floyd. We'll be in touch for the physical therapy details."

Samira managed to wait until they were out in the car before she let the tears come.

After a big hug, her dad said, "You know, you can still work out. You just can't put any strain on your shoulder."

"No beam," Samira sobbed. "No uneven bars. *Definitely* no vault."

"You can work on jumps and parts of the floor routine." Her dad pulled into the driveway and looked over at her. "Come on, honey. Let's make this work."

"I don't want to make it work!" Samira yelled and ran into the house.

She pounded up the stairs to her room. Samira knew she was acting like a baby, but in that moment she didn't care. She'd be brave later. Right now, she just wanted to cry.

* * *

Samira gingerly leaned over the mat laid out on the floor of the garage. Six months had passed, and Dr. Floyd had given her the green-light to start training again.

"Come on, try it!" Penelope sat cross-legged on top of an old dresser in the corner. Samira reached for a cartwheel and again, she felt the ache in her shoulder. Something was wrong. Something was off. Every time she put that twisting pressure on her shoulder, it felt like her muscles were turning to jelly. Her dad had even dragged her back to Dr. Floyd, but the doctor said the shoulder looked perfectly sound. "Sometimes joints are never quite the same as they once were," she said.

Samira wanted to punch the wall. Instead, she forced herself through the cartwheel. But at the top, she just couldn't hold it. That familiar weightless, flipping feeling was gone.

She wobbled, then stumbled down to the mat. "Pen, what's wrong with me?" she moaned. "My shoulder just doesn't feel the same. Everything feels off. Now it's not just my legs. Nothing works!"

"Your brain still works." Penelope hopped off the dresser and crawled across the mat to lay beside Samira. Together they stared at the ceiling. "Practice starts next week," Penelope said.

"Don't remind me." Samira sighed and crossed her hands on her chest. "I don't know." She forced out the words that had been building in her since her last visit to Dr. Floyd. "I don't know if I can go back with my shoulder like this."

"Nooo! You can't leave me! I can't get through pull-ups without you!" Penelope cried, half-jokingly.

Samira snorted laughter, but tears were building at the corners of her eyes. She didn't trust herself to speak.

CHAPTER 3

THANKS, BUT NO THANKS

Samira could tell something was up as soon as her parents came into her room that night. "What?" she asked, warily putting down her gymnastics scrapbook.

Mom's face held some secret surprise. "Well honey, Dad and I know how disappointed you are with your shoulder rehab. So we decided we all need a break—a fun break."

"We're going . . . snowboarding!" Dad whipped a piece of paper out from behind his back.

Gingerly, Samira took it. "Big Bear Family Snowboard Clinic" screamed the letters across the top.

"Ugh," she said, putting down the paper. "I mean, thanks. But –"

"And we're booked for next week!" Mom broke in. She leaned forward and kissed Samira on the forehead. "Trust us, sweetie. This is going to be fantastic."

Samira mom's smile was so big it lit up the room. Her dad's hazel eyes twinkled behind his glasses. Samira wasn't sold on this snowboarding vacation idea, but it was really nice of them. And maybe some time away from gymnastics was just what she needed.

* * *

Three days later, Samira found herself staring down a long ski slope, a snowboard strapped to her feet, a helmet on her head, and an instructor named Porter beside her. The pine-scented breeze slapped her cheeks, and the sun turned the snow into a blanket of glitter. The chalky air of the gym seemed a million miles away.

"All right, Samantha, remember that your board is your friend," Porter said, adjusting his own goggles.

"It's Samira,'" she corrected him through gritted teeth. "And I don't want to be here."

"Samira," he said agreeably. "Sorry. My bad. So here's what we're going to do. We'll just coast down together, okay? To get started, bend your knees, hold your arms out to the side, and tip your board a little bit down."

At least she knew how to do that. Balance. She could still balance. Porter watched as she leaned forward. "Nice!" he shouted as she started to move. He followed, catching up until they were side-by-side. "Beginners usually don't catch on so fast," he called.

"I'm a gymnast," she called back. "Balance is kind of my thing." She kept her eyes up and her core tight.

"Now try leaning to the right to turn a little right and left to turn a little left," Porter instructed as they slid past a stand of pine trees. "Your board will turn the way your body turns. Pressure on your board from your toes will turn your board toeside. Pressure from your heels will turn you heelside."

Samira tried and her board responded. The snow flew up in little sprays on either side. They were gathering speed, but she didn't feel afraid. She felt good.

"You're doing great!" Porter said as they coasted to a stop. "Want to try a little jump?"

"Yeah!" she said. And all of a sudden, she realized she meant it. She was surprised to be having this much fun.

"Okay. Unclip and follow me."

Samira leaned down and fumbled with the clips holding her boots to her board. She finally released them and tucked her board under her arm to follow Porter to another run nearby.

"Clip back in and listen up," Porter said. "The most important thing to remember with jumps is you have to commit. Once you're on the slope, you can't chicken out. That's how people get hurt. You have to go for it."

Just like gymnastics, Samira thought. Every gymnast knew that if you didn't commit to a routine, you were guaranteed to mess up.

"You're going to drop in—that means start to move forward—and glide down toward the jump. Aim for the middle, obviously," Porter said. "Knees bent, back straight, eyes up, arms out a little. The jump's going to shoot you into the air. Don't fight it. Go for it. When you land, bend your knees a lot to absorb the impact. Then just keep gliding. Try not to stop yourself—that's how people fall. They hit the brakes right after a jump."

Samira shifted impatiently. "Okay, I'm ready," she said. All this talking was making her even more eager to go.

"Go for it!" Porter said.

She tipped her board forward and dropped in. The board cut against the snow—*shussshh*!

"Lean forward to increase your speed! It's coming up!" Porter called.

Samira leaned forward and the *shushing* noise of the board sped up. The wind blew back against her face. Feeling her body fluid, in motion again, felt like a homecoming. Her legs felt strong, her muscles engaged.

Ahead, the jump lay like a wide ledge across the slope. *Commit*, she thought and leaned forward, spreading her arms wider. As her board hit the upslope of the jump, she pulled her legs up under her instinctively.

Her body soared through the air. That feeling of weightlessness—it was like flying on the uneven bars. *Bend your knees and stick the landing*, she told herself, just as her board hit the slope. She rocked back a little, then got her balance as she coasted down the slope. Samira sheared to a stop beside Porter, who had glided down to meet her.

"Wow!" Samira gasped as she took off her helmet and shook back her damp hair.

"That's what I was gonna say! You're a natural," Porter grinned. "Fun, right?"

"Yeah, fun," she echoed. Her legs were shaking in that good way you always get after a hard workout. It seemed like the fog had cleared out of her brain for the first time since the accident. She took a deep breath, and the chilly air seemed to clear her lungs. She turned to Porter, who was bent over, undoing the clasps on his board.

"When can I go again?" she asked.

CHAPTER 4

SLALOM SLOPES

"Okay, get ready! Let's shave some time off this slalom course!" Porter shouted two months later. Samira lowered her goggles and wiggled her board in the snow. If anyone had told her eight weeks ago that she would stop doing gymnastics and join the Big Bear Snowboard Junior Team instead, she would have laughed.

But here she was, and the race was the day after tomorrow. She looked down the slope, with its gates looming beneath her. "We can do this!" Samira's teammate Norah shouted beside her. They'd be racing together, head-to-head. The rest of the team was milling around at the bottom after their own runs.

Samira worked her hands deeper into her gloves. The wind whipped her face, but nothing got through her ski jacket and heavy padded pants. Briefly, she thought of the tight leotard and hair bun of gymnastics and the way her head always ached after a day of competition with her hair yanked back.

Porter hit the buzzer and Samira dropped her board onto the slope. Out of the corner of her eye, she could see Norah in her bright blue parka doing the same. She looked forward and could see nothing except the slope ahead, with the bright orange flags marking the gates.

Samira leaned into the first turn. Then she wove around another gate and then another. Her leg muscles pushed her up and over slopes, and then she glided down. A serpentine turn sent her up onto the banked side of the course, the snow spraying up beneath her board. Again, she soared back down the side of the bank, fast. Suddenly, she biffed, pinwheeling her arms until she felt herself steady—back on track. Gate, turn, gate, turn, then the final jump loomed. Norah, where was Norah? No time to look around, there wasn't any blue parka ahead.

Samira slammed the final jump, keeping her body over the board and slightly rotating her arms the way Porter had taught her. "Yeah!" she heard their teammate Georgia yell. Then came that sliding feel of her board hitting the snow, the spray in her face, and the crunch as she slowed to a stop. Norah slid up beside her a few seconds later.

"Nice jumps, girls!" Harper said.

Panting, Samira and Norah pushed up their goggles. Norah leaned over with her hands on her knees. Samira leaned down and unclipped her boots, then stepped out of her board. She walked in a slow circle with her hands behind her head. Blood and adrenaline were pumping through her. The air felt crisp and clean in her lungs.

"Good clean run, ladies!" Porter coasted up beside them. "Everyone get back up to the top—let's go again!" He turned to Samira. "You burned four seconds off your personal best. Excellent!"

"I felt strong," Samira said.

"You *are* strong." Porter motioned for her to jump onto the chairlift. "Lower-body muscle strength is really helpful when you want to keep the turns as close as possible through the gates."

Norah hopped onto the chairlift beside Samira. As they moved slowly up the mountain with their boards dangling, Norah sighed. "Porter's right. That was really good. I wish I could get air like you do."

"You do get air!" Samira told her.

"I know. I just need more muscle. You've already got it."

Samira thought of how her legs and hips always felt like a burden in the gym—like something extra that she'd be glad to get rid of. But here, on the slopes, they were her power. Samira no longer cursed her body and how she was built. She embraced it.

CHAPTER 5

GYM JITTERS

"Do you want to room together at Powder Basin?" Norah asked as they hiked back to the cars where their parents were waiting.

"Yeah! I can't believe we get to fly for our very first race," Samira said. "Are you nervous?"

"Kind of. Excited too. I know I can do it—I just want to be there, you know?" Norah ran toward her mom's car. "See you tomorrow!"

"Hi, honey," Samira's dad greeted her, as she climbed into the car. "Good practice? We've got to stop by the gym real quick. I need to drop off a check to Coach Hosseni for your last session."

Samira's dad talked on and on in the front seat as she tried to control her thoughts. Did he say they were going to the gym? The gym! She hadn't seen Coach or anyone except Penelope since the day of her accident. She looked down at her legs in their heavy padded pants and her ski boots. Was she really going to walk in there, dressed like a snowboarder? What would they all think?

"Dad, I think I'm just going to stay in the car," she announced as her father pulled up in front.

"What?" Her dad was already halfway out. "Come say 'Hi,' to everyone! I know they'll be dying to see you."

With her stomach sinking, Samira climbed out of the car and walked through the big blue doors as she had so many times before.

The smells hit her first—warm rubber, chalk, sweat. She could almost feel the dry, slippery feeling of chalk on her hands. She imagined the rubber mat squeaking under her feet and the hard leather of the beam.

"Samira!" Penelope streaked toward them like a blur in a purple leotard. "What are you doing here? I can't believe it! Are you ready to come back?" Then she stepped back as the others gathered around.

Coach Hosseni gave her a warm smile and stepped away to talk to Samira's dad.

"Um, hi! Yeah, I've been snowboarding a lot to stay in shape. Just while my shoulder gets better." She felt immediately as if she'd been disloyal. She hadn't really quit gymnastics. She had just stopped going.

"Yay! Then you're coming back, right?" Penelope said.

Samira blinked and looked around at the waiting faces. The silence stretched out. "Oh, of course!" she finally said.

"I can't wait!" Penelope hugged her. "I bet you'll kill those landings on the beam now that you've had time off."

Samira swallowed. A bad feeling was starting to rise in her throat as she pictured herself on the beam—trying, falling, struggling back on. She didn't want to feel that way anymore. Then she looked at Penelope's happy face and the gym with all of its fun, familiar apparatus. It was like coming home. She just didn't know if she really wanted to move back in.

CHAPTER 6

STICK IT!

"Samira, I've still got a place for you on the team," Coach Hosseni said, startling Samira out of her thoughts. Dad was beaming at her. That must have been what they were talking about. "If you want it, of course."

"Of course she wants it!" Penelope shrieked. "Yay! Sam! You're back in!"

"Oh! I . . ." Samira looked down at her jacket and boots. She felt terribly overheated. "Maybe . . ."

"I just have to know for sure," Coach Hosseni went on. "I've got a girl on the waiting list, and I promised I'd tell her tomorrow if there's a spot for her. I know she's very eager, so I don't want to keep her waiting."

Penelope grabbed her arm. "Can you stay? Do you want to work out on the beam with me? Please?"

"Go on, honey," Dad said. "I'll swing by and get you in an hour or so."

Fifteen minutes later, wearing one of Penelope's old leotards, Samira felt like she had stepped back in time. Her snowboarding life was gone. She was facing the beam. Up top, Penelope did a backflip and landed, arms out, wobbling a bit.

"Whooaa," she called, laughing. "Okay, now it's your turn. You've got this, Samira! I know you can do it!"

Samira mounted the beam, her heart hammering. "I'm nervous about my shoulder," she called down to Penelope.

"It'll be fine!" Penelope called up.

Samira took a deep breath and raised her arms, lifting her foot, she swung into the cartwheel. As her weight came into her hands, she felt her shoulder twinge. It held, but she swung her hips too far to the right and stumbled off the beam. As she brushed her hands off, she took a few deep, long breaths.

"That wasn't bad," Penelope said.

"Yeah . . ." Samira made sure she didn't cry before she said anything more. "Listen, this feels just sort of off. I guess I'm just not used to it anymore. Maybe I need more practice first."

"Well, sure, of course." Penelope gave her a little squeeze. "That makes sense."

Coach Hosseni came up beside them.

"Samira, have you tried any floor work? Let's see a few back flips," she said.

With her heart pounding, Samira followed Coach over to the floor mats. Penelope's leotard was a size too small. It cut into the tops of her legs. She tried to yank it down as she positioned herself at the corner of the huge mat.

"Remember, a strong take off will reduce the strain on your shoulder," Coach called. "Don't be afraid of the speed."

Vaguely, Samira was aware that the others had gathered at the edges of the mat, watching. She took two deep breaths, then ran, arms pumping. She bounded into the flip, arms extended, and then suddenly, everything snapped into place. Her hands thumped the mat, then her legs, knees bent, then hands again, legs, and hands. She heard Penelope call, "Stick it!" and she was done, upright at the corner of the mat.

The others burst into applause as she looked around, panting. "Wow!" Coach called. "This is Samira after a shoulder injury? Way to go!"

"Thanks," Samira said. She couldn't keep the grin off her face. It felt good when everything just worked. She'd kind of forgotten about that.

Her dad appeared at the gym doors and walked toward them, smiling. The other gymnasts scattered away to the beam, the bars, and the vault.

"Well, how did it go?" he asked.

"She did great!" Coach Hosseni told him. "You just missed her doing some fantastic backflips."

"How does your shoulder feel?" Samira's dad asked.

"Pretty good, actually," Samira admitted. "It was fun."

"Let me know by tomorrow night if you're still on the team," Coach said as the three of them strolled toward the doors. "I really have to know by then. Morning after that at the absolute latest."

"Yeah, I will," Samira assured her. But as she and her dad headed for the car, she had a terrible feeling in her stomach. She had a decision to make—whether to give her heart to the slopes or to the gym. Either way, she'd be leaving a little bit of herself behind.

CHAPTER 7

BACK ON THE BOARD

Samira dropped her board into the powder and sailed slowly down the gentle slope. Beside her, Norah turned left and right, cutting dreamy half-circles in the trail. They were the only ones out on the backcountry trail. Normally they'd need an adult to go with them, but this easy slope was the one closest to the ski center. Porter had told them they'd need to be back in half an hour.

For now, Samira wasn't thinking about time limits of any sort. She didn't want to think about anything. She felt the cold wind against her cheeks and the warmth of her hands in their gloves. Dark pine trees lined both sides of her. The air was crisp and smelled of evergreen. There was just something about a snowy trail at night.

They coasted down the trail, riding easily over the natural bumps and dips. The only sound was the *shush-shush* of their boards over the powdery snow. A log, bolstered by snow, lay in front of them—a natural jump.

"Come on, let's do it!" Samira called to Norah.

"Yeah!" her friend responded. Samira slowed down to let Norah go in front of her. Then she approached the jump herself, first aiming, then letting her board lift her into the air, just like Porter had taught her.

Then came that heart-stopping moment when her board went airborne. Just like in the gym, for an instant, she was weightless. Then her board hit the snow, and she was over it.

The girls looked at each other and laughed, both breathless. Then Samira slid to a stop as the trail petered out.

"Whew!" She sat down on a nearby log. Norah sat beside her and offered her a drink from the water bottle she was carrying in a small backpack. Between the trees, they could see the distant, colorful figures of their teammates sliding down the runs. If Samira listened hard, she could just make out their voices shouting to each other.

"So, guess what?" Samira said after she took a long swallow of water. "I went back to the gym yesterday."

"You did?" Norah lowered the water bottle and looked at her. "Why?"

"My dad had to drop off a check. But you won't believe what happened while I was there." She quickly filled Norah in on the impromptu practice session and Coach saying she still had a spot on the team. She described how good it felt to be at the gym.

"Wait, she said you had a spot still?" Norah asked, her forehead wrinkled. "But you said no, right? I mean, you're doing this now."

"Yeah." Samira looked down at the snow. "I am doing this now."

"And you can't do both," Norah said.

"No, that would be crazy. It's way too much," Samira said, looking down.

"So you told them no, right?" Norah stuck the water bottle back in her pack. "Obviously. The race is tomorrow—our first one! You can't quit on us now!"

Samira was silent. She didn't look up. She knew if she did, she'd see Norah's wide, worried eyes.

Norah sat back on the log. "Wait a minute. You didn't tell them no."

"No!" Samira said. "I mean yes! I mean—I don't know! I didn't say anything yet. But Coach said I have to decide by tonight. Someone else wants the spot otherwise."

"Huh. Well, what are you going to tell her?" Norah asked.

Samira sighed. "I don't know. I mean, listen, when I was back there, at the gym, it was like . . . I don't know, going back to camp or something. You know, when everything seems so familiar and you know where everything is and there's a million memories stuffed into every corner?"

Norah was nodding. "Yeah. I do." She paused and added, "I guess I just really like having you on *this* team."

"So do I," Samira said. "That's the problem." She gestured around her. "Like, here I am, sitting on a log, in the snow, and I'm so happy out here. I love the fresh air. I love just soaring down the slopes—it's *free* in a way that gymnastics isn't, know what I mean?"

Norah nervously asked, "So what are you saying? Are you going with the old familiar or the new fresh?"

Samira stood up and looked toward the team in the distance. She took a deep breath, the air burning her lungs all the way down. "The race is tomorrow."

"That's not exactly an answer." Norah stood up and clipped back into her board.

Samira stood up too. She stepped on her board and fastened the clips. Suddenly, her body ached to be on the slopes. She wanted to fly.

"Race you back!" she called out to Norah and pushed off to zip down the slope toward her team.

CHAPTER 8

AT HOME ON THE POWDER

When the girls got back to the ski lodge, the weight of her decision hit Samira full force. All around her, the locker room was filled with excited chattering as the team pulled socks and boots and strapped on goggles. Everyone was talking about the race they were heading to the next day. Across the room, Norah was fixing her hair in a tight French braid. She had been a little less chipper on the way back to the lodge.

Finally, people started filing out. As the last few stragglers gathered their gear, Samira punched Coach Hosseni's number into her cell. She gripped the phone tightly as it rang in her ear.

"Samira?" Coach Hosseni's voice was friendly. "I had hoped to hear from you last night. But I'm so glad you called now. I did tell the other family to wait a little longer until I heard from you."

"Yeah, Coach, that's what I wanted to talk to you about," Samira said. She felt a lump rising in her throat already. She quickly slipped out of the locker room into the quiet of one of the bathroom stalls nearby. Now no one would see if she started crying. "I'm . . . I'm not coming back."

There was a long pause. "Ah," Coach finally said. "I see."

"Remember that story you told me about you and your sister and gymnastics?" Samira reminded her. "You were just like me with gymnastics, except I don't think I want to work through it."

After a pause that felt like forever, Samira went on. "I mean, I love gymnastics, but when my body doesn't cooperate, I get so stressed. Knowing I'll never have the right body build to go as far as I want makes me not want to do it anymore. With snowboarding, my build gives me the power and muscle I need. I love gymnastics and snowboarding, but I think I could go farther with snowboarding, and I want to try." There was another long silence. "Are you mad?"

"No! No, I'm not mad," Coach said. "I'm just thinking, that's all. I'm thinking how hard it must have been for you to say that. I bet it was a little—well, a lot—scary."

"Yes! I feel like I'm losing my family or my home or something." Samira squeezed the phone tight. Her hand was sweaty.

"You've found a new home." Coach's voice was gentle. "And one that fits you better. I understand. I will miss you, though."

"I'll miss you too, Coach," Samira answered. The lump was still sitting in her throat, but a huge weight melted off her shoulders.

"Now, there's someone else here, waiting," Coach Hosseni said. "I'm going to give her the phone."

"Samira?" Penelope said.

"Did you hear?" Samira squeezed her eyes shut, waiting.

"Yeah," Penelope said. "I'm sad."

"Are we still going to be friends?" Samira asked.

"What?" Penelope squawked. "Did you really think I'd drop my best friend just because you're not in gymnastics anymore?"

"No," Samira said. "Okay, maybe a little."

"Just because we're not in the same sport doesn't mean we're not friends anymore!" Penelope sounded comically outraged.

"Promise?" Samira sighed with relief.

"Yeah! Of course. Now go out and grab some air or whatever they say in snowboarding."

"You mean catch some air?" Samira laughed.

"Yeah, that. I'll text you later, okay?"

"Okay."

When Samira hung up the phone, the lump in her throat had disappeared.

* * *

The next day was a flurry of activity, but Samira felt good about her decision. When the buzzer sounded for the race, Samira felt like she'd never been more ready for anything in her life. She felt strong. Her head was clear.

Samira dropped in fast and whipped around the first gate. She swooped up on the turn, then back down to the next gate, then a fast one, two, three. She whipped her board so close to the poles she almost brushed them as the cheering from the crowd at the bottom filled her ears. She could feel her legs controlling the board, her muscles fighting hard to keep her straight and upright. She was a machine and every part was working.

She rounded the final gate and then hit the last jump. The huge, white ramp was all she could see. Samira soared up and twisted her board back and forth to keep steady.

She hit the snow, with the powder spraying up and then the finish line, blue against the white snow. Samira coasted to a stop and leaned over, her hands on her knees. She'd done it—her first race. She was a snowboarder now. And there was no going back.

Author Bio

Emma Carlson Berne has written more than a dozen books for children and young adults, including teen romance novels, biographies, and history books. She lives in Cincinnati, Ohio with her husband, Aaron, her son, Henry, and her dog, Holly.

Illustrator Bio

Since graduating from Loughborough University School of Art and Design in 2004, Katie Wood has been a freelance illustrator. From her studio in Leicester, England, she creates bright and lively illustrations for books and magazines all over the world.

GLOSSARY

apparatus (a-puh-RA-tuhs)—equipment used in gymnastics, such as the balance beam or vault

backcountry (BACK-kuhn-tree)—an isolated area that is not marked by trails or patrolled by park rangers or other authorities

chairlift (CHAIR-lift)—a line of chairs attached to a moving cable that carries people to the top of a mountain or ski hill

drop in (DRAHP IN)—to start a snowboard run

gate (GAYT)—one of many plastic poles, sometimes with flags, that snowboarders and skiers must go around

heelside (HEEL-side)—the edge of the board closest to a snowboarder's heels

impromptu (im-PRAHMP-too)—unplanned

serpentine (SUR-pen-teen)—an S-shaped or winding path

shear (SHEER)—to cut off sharply

slalom course (SLAH-luhm COURS)—a snowboarding course in which the competitor must ride between poles or flags, requiring quick, sharp turns

toeside (TOE-side)—the edge of the board closest to a snowboarder's toes

DISCUSSION QUESTIONS

1. Samira has a hard choice to make in this book—how to choose between two sports she loves. Think of a time when you were asked to choose between people, activities, pets, or friends. What happened? What strategies did you use to help make your choice?

2. At the end of the book, Samira explains her decision to Coach Hosseni. What are the reasons she gives for choosing snowboarding over gymnastics? Look back through the book and give specific examples from the text that support Samira's reasons.

3. Both Penelope and Norah are supportive friends to Samira. Look back through the book. Make a list of three ways that these friends help Samira. Now think of a time when you felt supported, by a teacher, coach, parent, sibling, or friend. How did this person help you?

WRITING PROMPTS

1. Samira must decide between gymnastics and snowboarding. At the end of the book, she chooses snowboarding. Imagine a scenario in which Samira makes the opposite choice. What would happen if she chose to go back to the gym instead? Write that scene as a different ending for this book.

2. Samira's parents think that going to the ski slopes will be fun. Imagine a conversation between Samira's mom and dad in the kitchen before they show Samira the flier. What do they say to each other? Write their dialogue.

3. Go forward a year in time and write a letter from Samira to Penelope, describing her snowboarding life. What has changed for Samira since the end of the book? What is the same? Use your imagination!

MORE ABOUT
SNOWBOARDING

Snowboarding started with a surfer. In 1965, a surfer named Sherman Poppen wanted to try building a surfboard for the snow. He bolted together two plastic skis and let his daughter Wendy try out his new invention.

The first snowboards cost about fifteen dollars. People called them "snurfers" (snow surfers) and considered them more of a toy than a piece of sports equipment.

In the early 1980s, before snowboarding became widely accepted, many ski resorts wouldn't allow snowboarders on their slopes. They were considered too wild.

At the 1982 National Snow Surfing Competition in Vermont, the starting gate was made of an upturned kitchen table and at the end, riders crashed into hay bales to stop their runs.

Men's and women's snowboarding made their Olympic debut in 1998 at the Nagano Winter Games. Canadian Ross Rebagliati took home the first ever snowboarding Olympic gold medal when he won the men's giant slalom event by 0.02 seconds.

In 2018, snowboarder Chloe Kim became the youngest female snowboarder to win Olympic gold when she dominated the halfpipe event at the PyeongChang Winter Games. She was only seventeen at the time.

The vast majority of snowboards are still made by hand. Strips of wood are glued together, then sandwiched between layers of fiberglass.

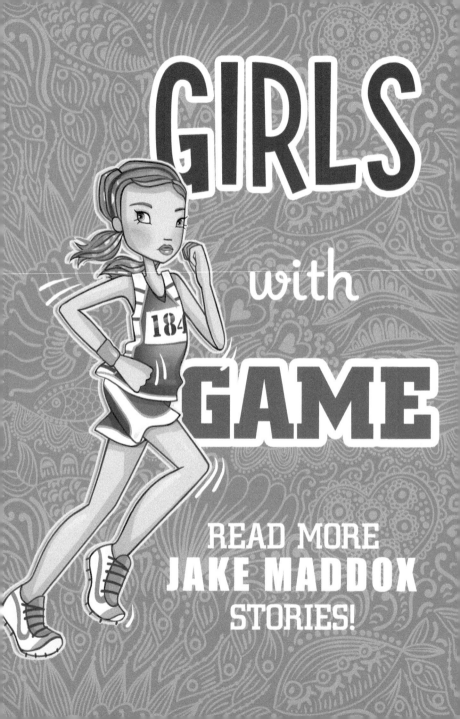

GIRLS

with

GAME

READ MORE
JAKE MADDOX
STORIES!

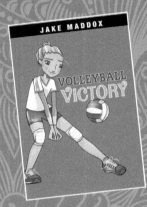

JAKE MADDOX

VOLLEYBALL VICTORY

JAKE MADDOX

COWGIRL Grit

JAKE MADDOX

SOCCER SURPRISE

JAKE MADDOX

REBOUND TIME

JAKE MADDOX

LONGBOARD Letdown

JAKE MADDOX

STRIKER'S SISTER

JAKE MADDOX

Digging DEEP

JAKE MADDOX

Pool PANIC

JAKE MADDOX

SQUAD STRUGGLES

KEEP THE SPORTS ACTION GOING...

DISCOVER MORE JAKE MADDOX BOOKS AT

capstonepub.com!